VENEETA SINGHA

Gazes Untold

A Novel

First published by REEDSY 2024

Copyright © 2024 by Veneeta Singha

All rights reserved. No part of this publication may be reproduced, stored or transmitted in any form or by any means, electronic, mechanical, photocopying, recording, scanning, or otherwise without written permission from the publisher. It is illegal to copy this book, post it to a website, or distribute it by any other means without permission.

This novel is entirely a work of fiction. The names, characters and incidents portrayed in it are the work of the author's imagination. Any resemblance to actual persons, living or dead, events or localities is entirely coincidental.

Veneeta Singha asserts the moral right to be identified as the author of this work.

Veneeta Singha has no responsibility for the persistence or accuracy of URLs for external or third-party Internet Websites referred to in this publication and does not guarantee that any content on such Websites is, or will remain, accurate or appropriate.

First edition

This book was professionally typeset on Reedsy. Find out more at reedsy.com

Contents

Chapter 1	1
Chapter 2	7
Chapter 3	13
Chapter 4	19
Chapter 5	25
Chapter 6	32
Chapter 7	40
Chapter 8	49
Chapter 9	58
Chapter 10	66

Chapter 1

a falsis principiis proficisci

The clock tower was an impassive relic of a medieval martial regime remembered as a symbolic destiny, a flowing cascade of the true Asiatic value system, a history for the senses. A cornerstone of land-marked navigability, it was held up by many minds in the manner of a bestowal rather than a functional presence. Others would, however, look at its simple mechanics with annoyance and an interrupted mentality. "The day will come when this citadel sees a new horizon," Razi said to the taxi driver as she strode into a taxi, troubled again by the incessant crowding near the clock tower. The driver pointed to the meter and started the vehicle with a tired expression. Had the pavement appeared any less new, the day's frenetic pace would have decided on negation instead of a quiet movement into familial surroundings. The road meandered around the city with a near-sardonic recognition of bumps and broadness. The park seemed greened and empty. Razi sighed with relief and looked outside at the city spaces while the taxi swerved through the traffic. "This route is unusually smooth today." She said to the taxi driver after they passed the bridge near the city's southern perimeter. He smiled, nodded and rolled up his window quickly. Any reigning trope on kindred spirits would have explained the driver's beaming expression. Yet, the stumbling reticence that city denizens felt and showed among each other was the winner, an arc against inevitable recalcitrance, salvation itself.

The statue at the front of the arcade had been polished for the upcoming festival. While the driver was careful not to look sideways, Razi faced the window and looked at the homage with a lingering sense of indecision. "Do they know who built the arcade or is that just a showpiece these days?" She murmured as the driver turned to look at her. "Well, historical figures are important for us all." He replied grinning and cruising his taxi into a wooded lane. They reached Razi's home in a moody farewell despite the summer's unabating heat and overcrowded alleys. "Thank you," Razi said as she paid the driver and opened the small, iron-crusted gate to her home. The small bower of bougainvillaea was flush with blooming pinks. The sight brought tears to her eyes and she felt a day's crude troubles ease away in a momentary flash of colour. The taxi moved away without a sound but an acknowledged understanding was evident. The city would not become a burden to her nor her newfound compatriot. It was a longstanding argument for better habitability that had run its course and found far too much sinister causality along the way. The mayor's office had given Razi a final sign-off and approval which, in turn, had freed her

CHAPTER 1

from the daily motions of overwork. "Business as usual, then?" Her young neighbour shouted to her from behind the adjoining fence while she walked in through the front door.

An unplanned day arose the next morning with Razi sifting through her boxed belongings for much of the afternoon. Piled office folders had assumed the dubious position of deterrence rather than daily reminders. She found a chiffon shirt that she had not worn which was also a gift from her school friend. Among other forgotten valuables, she saw a beautiful golden hair brush and mirror set inside one of her suitcases that was still shiny and untouched. She stopped for a moment, thinking of her close friendships of the past which were now, simply, sacrificed bonds. Razi was an accomplished business professional with many accounts to her credit yet she was equally aware of the need for a less office-bound life. As a business coach, she would draft out many downsides to the profession and defer the rest from the tutorship with incisive intelligence. Professionals in business systems were always keen to bring her into some imminent intractability and would, thereafter, find measurements towards advancing ideas instead.

***

The dim lights in her newly-renovated kitchen elicited a wistful energy and she decided to spend more time at home. Her husband had cautiously placed a glistening tray with a porcelain vase on the counter table. Perhaps it was a maudlin resignation to a duality that persisted in their lives. He was in a foreign placement for the rest of the year and it took less than a day of his absence for Razi to realise that she would have to see her impromptu plans through at all cost. The running joke in her neighbourhood was that business could be unusual in the summertime but it should be pleasant during cloud bursts. Stagnant and undone, the floundering town economies were swept clean by new growth politics and high levels of capital infusion. Razi looked outside her kitchen window and saw a small fig tree sprout its branches towards her side of the fence. Was this an admonition too, much in the way her wayfaring city would sound off alarm bells in less than obvious ways?

Razi was a strong-minded woman, thoroughly melded into many societal and professional upsurges which others had keeled under over the years. Determined not to allow mindless sociability into her small sphere, she had preserved remnants of the Nepali norm with a smiling demeanour. Yet, today she felt an overwhelming urge to cut away a knotted past, to breathe without anxious thought, to allay her early awakenings. The telephone rang jolting her out of a long-delayed introspection. "We have a few hours to decide what to pack and what to lock away, madam," The transportation service chief said in a lighthearted tone. "Thank you, *Dai*. I was thinking of locking away the rush and my crowded commutes too." Razi replied feeling relieved and unburdened by the conversationality. "We will leave on Sunday but you can reschedule anytime. Give me a ring if plans change." With this, the chief hung up, yet, for Razi, it felt as though many doors had opened to unlocked possibility, a counter-exposure, an afternoon's collusion reinvented. She called her compadre next door and said, "I'll be going out of town for a bit. The house will be locked but it'd be wonderful if you could keep a lookout while I'm away." Jor was not surprised by the news but he replied quickly, "Of course, *Didi*. Why don't we meet tomorrow over coffee? I have some work I need help with, too." Overturning the stress-induced sociability of her working life, Razi calculated her final move away from the city in small steps of actualisation. "That would be super, Jor. Halse will not be here for the next two years but I must figure out a way to live better." It was a curious resolution that had been handed to many city denizens because of their perseverance and continuing leadership.

The city skyline was vivid in the late afternoon with puffs of cloud covering the firmament in message-like formations. She sat on her mother's favourite cane chair in the veranda and jotted down a list of reminders, looking at the changing skies every now and then. "We've got some fruit trees in the garden now, Razi." shouted a voice from nearby. Razi down from the veranda and saw her young neighbour laughing at a red plastic bucket tucked away under yet another fruit tree. "Did you plant it?" Razi asked, laughing in unison. The young boy shook his head and plucked a small fruit to taste it. "It is time for the system to return to old values again," Razi said unthinkingly as though signs of precarious living were subsumed by the city's inertia. She watched the young boy fill the bucket with the small fruit and keep it in a corner. He waved out to her and walked into his home. Halse, her husband, would have punished the young truant, but she suddenly found the scene somewhat enlightening. Having lived in the city periodically, she could sense change and changelessness without much effort. But, the years ahead were certain to be less divided, more just, divergent. She sat on the chair and wrote a few more reminders with ease. The years had moved slowly and painstakingly as though time would leave no stone unturned for the city. It was now a season for selfhood, serenity, sense-making of a personal kind.

***

Chapter 2

a minore ad maius

Tareni was a city in the making, resonant in recent years as a city away from the city and an urban vision. It was a sprawling township too, resolved by the habitation imperative and a determined move towards restraint. "A lot has been accomplished in Tareni since I was there last, Halse. I will be comfortable in my new role as a teacher too." Razi said to her husband over the telephone while he listened with a hopeful smile. "The mayor's desk is fully apprised now. I can return to the city works when you come back home." She finished her conversation with a pleased mind. "Well, you certainly can take care of yourself, Razi. Give my fondest to our friends in Tareni." Halse replied and returned to his breakfast. A shiny reflection of the sun's rays on the window pane brought an untimely warning, a plain remembrance, the final opening to another human cosmology. She stood near this reflection and recounted, to herself, the early years of her working life. It had been a jostle as much as it had been an entry point. She looked at her empty desk, but the poignant sun did not leave its promise half-fulfilled. She walked towards her cupboard and took out cardigans and new clothing in a hurried awareness of not having enjoyed a fashionable life for a long time. She was not extravagant about her needs and her family would often refurbish Halse and her home with many necessities. There were boxes near the table, tied and untouched, that she did not remember. She looked at a small, old one in fright. Opening the box was a course for new success because she did not hoard nor consume in an obvious way.

Clutching a beautiful mohair cardigan in her hands, Razi looked around apprehensively. The room was bright and fresh with Halse's strict reminders stamped on it. Time was gradual and deliberate in the city when she sat down to collect her thoughts. Her cousins were quick to jumpstart her flagging social life every time they met. Now it was but natural that Razi stepped out of a city's curriculated existence and found a softer approach. Her guide and supervisor had finished his ardent business engagements and returned to the village for good. Widespread changes in habitation were usually met with simple rationality by many in her immediate realm. She was beginning to see the wisdom and forethought behind much of her community's self-imposed but understated resistance. With the cardigan in her hands, she strode to the living room and switched on the lamp to see this brand-new recreation of an older, untested Nepali familiarity. It looked soft and silken under the lampshade and reminded Razi of her youth. A friend had sent it to her as a sample from a new business venture with a jovial note on their collective yet variegated work ethic. "This is not a fruit of our labour but a symbol of triumphant labour." The note was written by hand and sealed with a characteristic signature. She found herself smiling at her friend's candour and warmhearted nudge. The lampshade too had caused a small miracle in Razi's unrelenting pursuit of a viable working life.

"We will be reaching with a lighter load, madam. It's the least we can do for ourselves after those hectic years." The transportation chief himself arrived early on Sunday with a casual flair that struck the right chord. He had chosen a shiny minibus for their journey and seemed particularly proud of his wares. Somehow, an uncanny notion of a shared past seemed to pervade much of Razi's community conversations. "My suitcases are not heavy but Halse believes in being prepared. I have a lot of my belongings stuffed in." She said with a grin. She had thought the move through thoroughly but had not anticipated the journey's eventuality or decisiveness. As she entered the bus, she looked around at her fellow travellers and found a few smiling faces with which to share her trip. "I'm not afraid of the roads so much as the landslides they repost in the news." She said with a laugh as the rest watched her sit with a sigh. The journey began with a simple and silent farewell to their homes and yet it seemed as though a shift was imminent, artfully presented, destined for many. The road to Tareni was wide and smooth and the hillsides appearing near the bends became an absolute truth for Razi. She watched the scenery from the bus window with an overwhelming feeling of having discovered a metallic earth and the natural expression of temporality. There were a few homes and buildings lined along the roads seemingly reviving memory rather than culling habitation.

***

The small minibus wove a comic tale as the travellers watched the *terra firma* observe a certain diptych, an uncertain tension, a terse recognition. The road was newly tarred and heavy with not load but lightness. It was a momentary return yet they knew that the city would have to exist as the past and a present but never the future of claims and counterclaims. Razi smiled at intermittent stops while the roadside melee took over and the driver would look at his passengers to see if they had seen what he did not remember. "I wonder if the bus stop ever saw the bus clean the road. I did when I was young." One of the young travellers said loudly in a sudden burst of laughter. "We worry about journeys too much, Didi." He said looking at Razi as the bus heaved and they laughed together at this truism. The day had passed on the bus with very little to do except when someone would take out a sandwich or a tiffin box filled with food. "I saw a small restaurant somewhere. Perhaps, we could all stop for a hearty meal soon." Razi said in a soft voice to the driver and halted the journey's unending movement. "There's one up ahead. We can stop there." said the driver trying to remember the exact location of the restaurant. The passengers looked relieved and prepared to enjoy a local meal by the road that had been bypassed many times in their lives.

Sitting in a small but well-built restaurant near a local checkpoint, the bus group looked around with an unanticipated sense of place, eagerness, their mind's eye into the farthest reaches of the verdant area. It was past lunchtime but the restaurant was prepared for a rollout offering. A few timid and diffident looks at each other began to take root and the driver watched this new community with a huge smile. He was glad to be returning to Tareni and leaving behind his unending tussles and tensions. The group seemed to have gone back in time to their youth, perhaps on a bus ride to school, yet the place was firmly placed in the present and future rather than the past. Razi said after a while, "Tareni is not far, I see. We could sit together and enjoy this meal." The rest of the group looked at her with relief and gratitude and moved towards her table. "It is almost like moving into another plane of existence after leaving our crowded city. Although I am a city dweller, I wonder if reports of hidden worlds are true." Razi's bus partner said as she sat purposively on a ledge nearby. The uneven and rolling lands around the restaurant space did not impinge on their presence. Instead, the built environment was comfortably supported, extended in time, emblazoned by a natural enclosure. Razi and her travel companions smiled in agreement.

The restaurant meal had a local flair that was uncommon in the city. "The farmers' markets are stocked with wonderful products but I prefer this kind of authenticity." Razi's bus partner said again as they finished their meal and waited to go to the washroom. Razi laughed at this statement as though it had expressed, exactly, the momentary experiences of the travellers since the start of their journey. The restaurant manager walked towards them with a silver plate filled with dried fennel and *mishri*. "Thank you. I am like a well-fed country man today." The driver said, helping himself to a handful of the fennel and *mishri*. The day was barely noticeable except when the lilting landscape shifted and waned while the sun veered overhead. It was a distant place the travellers had chosen as their new destination yet it had now come to represent a quieting of many personal and professional dilemmas in their lives. "The time is right for the last leg of our trip. We can share many more meals in Tareni when we reach there." The driver's optimism shook off a hypertense awareness of change among his passengers. They boarded the minibus smiling at each other in a differentiated moment of companionship. A city was not the past nor was Tareni the future. In absolute sentience, Razi could understand that much lay ahead of her but she would find an appropriate way for herself.

***

Chapter 3

a solis ortu usque ad occasum

Tareni was awake, early in the morning, with bright awareness and a certain mood. The day ahead would not be recklessly exposed, wasteful, another strength enervated by denigration. Overvalued lands and undervalued property rights were fast becoming superior political issues to discuss and deny. Homes dotted around the small wave-like hill formations seemed to mirror this social anxiety. Razi had found her cousin's home without a single hitch. It was a low rent, for all intents and purposes. She sat on a comfortable dining room chair with the remaining rent papers and read them thoroughly. Was the rent sufficient for a city lifestyle to inhabit a wonderfully-preserved home? She thought to herself after the fine print had made its predictable impact and ensured a varying sort of contentment and contention. Razi's days were sure to be wound correctly around her choices yet there was much work to re-envision well into the years ahead. Scandalous details about property disputes would often emerge in the city and its neighbouring towns. Yet, the resolutions were lesser-known facts that rarely found ink or paper. Her uncle's long-standing contestation of basic rental principles was a childhood memory now. The days were not counted as a mere payment existence anywhere, any longer. The courts were not dusting off the files or file cabinets in a loose attempt to lock away troubles and people's losses. The raging political revolution within the district perimeters had found repairment well before the movement took hold of the streets and people's minds.

She pored over the papers for the next half hour, deciding on nothing but to firm up the daily details swiftly. Razi had fallen into the habit of maintaining efficiency above all else. The mechanical drudgery was not visible until her colleagues pointed it out in a humorous way. With drastic changes being wrought by her husband in their daily life, she had expected a break rather than a moving away, a plain passage, another determinant. Today, she felt comfortable in her aloneness and saw clearly what lay ahead of her. Tareni was her home now. Regardless of the disparities that were discussed by her circles, she was keen to be on even ground, to solve the equalisation, to surrender to no force. The imposition of workload after workload had transformed their offices. Many people had sought the prevalent socio-political reversion which had worked in Razi and her husband's favour. Now, a simpler world was imminent, residual, turning towards Razi too. The day had started with a haze of mist that Razi did not remember having seen for a long time. She stood up and walked into the back garden, looking at the small potted plants kept for her somewhat furtively. The blooms in the late afternoon showed signs of keen vitality and the mornings had kept the lushness intact. She looked over the fence and into the neighbour's large untended garden. The grass was unkempt yet an inevitable feeling of adverse life had dissipated into another era of pardons, unpardoned inversions, ablated intrusion.

Razi's morning routine paved the way for rooting out an infirmity which was rife amongst the city's dwellers. An uncertain weakness would surface in people's homes and lives that often led to illness, mental distress, a debilitating loss of strength. Suddenly, there was a heavy knock on the neighbour's door which Razi heard from the back garden. Loud voices did not ensue but, instead, an angry and high-pitched argument took over the morning's awakenings. She hurried into the kitchen and closed the door behind her in the hope that she would not be seen from nearby. The still eternity of a town's presence was Razi's chosen remembrance from her youth for many years and she wished there was more space, time and community for this exact atmosphere to re-emerge. The duelling neighbours had wrought a quiet end to their arguments but only they knew the true nature of this social destiny, this implosive message, the ensuing vulnerability. Razi sat at the kitchen table with a smile and a grimace. Tareni was sure to be a phase in her working life and so much more in an ordinary way. The town had impressed on her and her travel companions that a place could be new but the implacable nature of people would see them into lighter times and soluble differences. Lessened burdens were evident and Razi began to appraise her schedules and plans as though she were a supervisor rather than the appraised. This had become a time for unease to recoil into decision and impulse.

***

An everyday horror in the form of an old telephone made itself known to Razi the next day as she dressed for a day in Tareni's district area. She stood looking at this relic with no new association but that of an inverted systemic long denounced by its most avid champions. The speed dial era was a blessed escape from communicated disorders and failings of all tempos. She found herself smiling at the enforced havoc it had brought in its wake in the city with people locking it away as everything from a foreign implant to the devil's three-pronged fork. The day was sure to arrive when she would associate with her own place in decidedly new ways too but the city was not problematized by small trifles nor in simplistic complaisance. A personal choice and necessity had woven itself into an unexpected yet gratifying movement towards renewed livability. She giggled at the remembrances that the telephone had evoked as she walked out of the front door, resolved by better habitation rather than any personal decision. The day was still and placid with a few signs of marketplace activity interspersing the everyday details. She walked towards the taxi stand but decided to walk towards Tareni's shopping hub. The roads were tarred and ready while the stores and homes that lined them reverberated as solid structural entities. She looked around and wondered where her travel companions were and if she would meet them again. Tareni was much more than a city away from a city now. It was a home to be explored.

The afternoon sunshine was a warming influence when Razi

walked into a mid-size arcade with a restaurant inside. There were three floors bursting with goods of every imaginable preference and a booth at the centre. As Razi moved inside, the people near the booths and stores turned to look at her. Momentarily, the scene resembled a cinematic frame with Razi as the casual misconnection, a stumbling, a revocation of familiarity. She smiled icily at the people near the front booth and proceeded to the restaurant. They watched her intensely for a few minutes while she reached the restaurant and inquired about lunch. She was approached by a smiling young waitress who guided her to a comfortable table near the windows. In precise steps, Razi introduced herself to a new city and, in consonance, realized that Tareni too had shown her a nice spot for lunch. She felt oddly embarrassed by this yet vividly aware of the new surroundings and people. "Have you been to Tareni before?" asked the young waitress as she placed a tumbler of lemonade on the table. Razi could not articulate the right answer and had forgotten her visits at a much earlier time. She hesitated for a few minutes and looked at the waitress still smiling and waiting near the window. They laughed together, finally, and took the burden away from what ought to have been a wholesome community gathering. Razi quickly ordered her standard meal and looked around for more enquiring expressions. The restaurant was filled with eager lunch-goers and the day became a stamped recognition, rhetoric for the collective, a smile on many weary faces.

After finishing lunch, Razi strode around the ground floor peering into the amply stocked shops with eagerness. "Good afternoon, Didi," said a loud voice from the corner shop. The person was Razi's minibus companion who was sitting at the shop counter holding an elegant paper fan. Razi and her travel partner sat together and found a warm friendship in this cold arcade for the masses. "I will be living here on my own for a while. It is good to know that you are local and well-established. It takes a very long time to settle into any place much less a city like Tareni. I don't think I have made the wrong decision though. There are so many nice spots here." Razi said in a short breath, excited to have found a kindred spirit. Her newfound friend laughed loudly and pointed out many of Tareni's local necessities. "You have work in the days ahead?" She asked Razi while the arcade became less marbled and better lit. "Yes, but it will not be standard office work," Razi replied watching the space undo many false assumptions about living in a quieter realm, within difference, inside a built yet natural system. "I chose to take some time off too. I've worked hard my whole life believing I would reach a personal goal of some kind. I think it's safe to assume that I need not bother too much about it anymore." The words were reasonable and simply articulated but the conclusive nature of the thoughts and Razi's tone were deafening even for the arcade's casual strollers.

***

Chapter 4

absit iniuria

It was an early *Tihar* for Razi, one which would emerge rather than insert itself from a distance amidst many other priorities, events, spaces. Her family was happily ensconced at home and her cousins were sure to call her with happy smiles and conversation. For many decades, the last festival of the year was an unfathomable gathering in the city as many people absented themselves elsewhere and predicted, presented, purposively awaited a good winter. Razi's first few days in Tareni had morphed into a silent retreat while she woke up, every day, to a new stage in her life. She settled her files, accounts and financials in methodical steps that unearthed an unrecognised notion of changed times. Was she destined to close old chapters and stamp the new? After meeting a few familiar faces in her new home, she was unsure about her social life and if there would be any reconnections with the past. The office groups in the city were quick to cure Razi's grievances through lighthearted gatherings and a supportive atmosphere. Her early misgivings with waves within the re-established system had long been reworked within the office perimeters. Yet, a protracted, ulterior social debasement was present in the city's public realm. People would see this gashed consciousness wreak its violent milestones on city life and, mostly, the professional milieu. Often, there were hushed discussions on hostility itself as a strategic devaluation, derailment, a divisionary inequity that would further no cause but its own end.

The new evening had fallen on Razi's home in small descents of darkness as she sat in the kitchen, cutting freshly washed vegetables. The neighbourhood was not tightly packed but the homes seemed shadowy and shadowed by the day's end. She chopped the potatoes and the greens furiously, remembering to dip them in water before she placed them in a steel bowl. The greens were larger than she had seen for a long time. The rice cooker had made a silent re-entry into Razi's kitchen and was gurgling occasionally. The lentils were prepared the day before giving Razi another opportunity to revive her kitchen time. A knock on the kitchen door interrupted this meditative occasion and Razi's neighbour walked in carrying a large tray with a dish of roast chicken. "My husband made this for you, Raziji. Welcome to the neighbourhood." She said with a warm smile and laughed at Razi's visible surprise. "Thank you. I have not had the time to introduce myself. Please sit and have a glass of juice." The mechanical nature of Razi's city sociability had eased away but without any substitutes nor any planned circles. "I'm Ravi's wife, Shreela. It's nice to see that you are settling in. We moved here in the same way too." The neighbourhood appeared alive suddenly and Razi's anxieties abated with this new connection. The two ladies sat and exchanged a few more pleasantries that would soon bind the neighbourhood together in a strong way. "We have changed the padlocks but nothing else," Shreela said as she walked out of the door.

"It's an ethnic problem, Razi. We are stuck in an emptiness, not in any problem." Razi's cousin said with a firm grin as though this was just as much a revelation as it was a statement of discontent, disillusionment, distanced trauma. "Well, if it's an ethnic dilemma, it will be solved as one. Cultural deficits are tallied these days. I was surprised to see this at the Mayor's office. We have a lighter political sentence to decipher now." Razi replied hastily not wanting this conversation to end. For Razi, her cousin was a true compatriot but she was not fond of the city or its truant political mayhem. "You live a reclusive life that was always considered an authentic choice," Razi said again without much thought but with an overwhelming need to firm up their relationship in any way she could. Her cousin laughed and looked at Razi intently, insightfully, knowingly. "Many of us in the city wait for a wholesome break but it never occurs the way it should," Razi said handing her cousin a beautiful Chinese bowl that she had bought for her from the city. "Are you still cursing our deviance from the authentic Nepali way, Razi? Remember the school nurse who labelled you a rebel because of it?" Razi's cousin, Devi, said in a joyful tone, remembering their youth and the gaffes they were known for in school. The two sat in Devi's small but spacious terrace, for a long time, surrounded by Tareni's local spaces and keen natural atmosphere.

***

"I will be inviting Shreela for a nice lunch soon and, maybe, my new friend and neighbours too. What do you think?" Razi asked Halse over the telephone, eager to tell him about her days in Tareni. "You must and remember to explore the city before you dive into work. News from the city sounds better than I have known for a long time. The trade talks were upbeat." Halse replied as they discussed their plans with an optimism that was absent for many years. "I visited an arcade in town and it reminded me of all that we have lost to the city's new plans. I might even walk around today to see more of Tareni's hidden benefits." Razi said bringing a beaming smile to her husband's face. "I was worried, Razi, that the move to Tareni might not suit you. I think you'll enjoy the change." The conversation ended with a refreshing air of comfortable localness, homeliness, privacy. Halse was busy with work and could now rest easy knowing that Razi was settling in safely. After finishing the conversation, Razi sat on the front porch of the small home and began to write a series of notes and schedules. Halse was foremost in her mind while she put together many pages of personal and professional tasks, reminders and daily activities. It seemed like a peculiar and unfamiliar change for Razi, at first, that she was writing down many things that were hitherto habitual and undertaken instinctively. Would a better lifestyle emerge for her, she thought as she finished what she set out to do. In an odd sense, the hectic nature of city life had not disappeared but, instead, transmuted into a conscious will, a correlation, a well-sensed stepping into the future.

CHAPTER 4

Tareni's central district was an uneven promise of untraded markets, merchandise, milestones of happy necessity. Razi walked into one of the lanes lined with provision depots and smiled at a shop owner feeding biscuits to a stray dog. It was a new place, suddenly, for Razi that required a few steps of cautious familiarity to build up, one step at a time. Everyone in the district lanes was walking around too, keenly sizing up the wares against their needs and plans. She watched the rest discussing the day's marketing in every way possible. "The furniture looks polished, today, much more than a few days ago." She heard a man shout to his companion while she strolled in. She stopped to see some of the handicrafts displayed in a large showroom that almost carried with it an entire history of locality and tradition. She looked at a large carved table and wondered why her family and her colleagues seldom explored Nepali handicrafts the way many people in the city were known to. "Where was this made?" She asked the assistant in the showroom quietly. "Tareni, madam, Tareni," came the beaming reply. She looked up at the showroom assistant who was smiling at her and, then, at the table in a peculiar way. "I see." She said and walked towards the end of the lane.

The day in the city district passed away without warning back at home. Razi had bought stocks for the kitchen along with a large porcelain bowl. Settling into the large sofa in the living room, she turned on the television after a long time to watch the news. The Nepali news reader on one of the channels announced the day's events in a slow, droning voice. She had planned to warm up dinner after the news but decided to watch television until eight o'clock. Tareni's local channel was a voluble remix of local programming and terse news relays. The day had been fruitful and enjoyable with Razi finding her way around her new city. It was time for her to move ahead and resume the work she had promised to finish. The night sky in Tareni was starlit, sensed by sight, silvery in its timing. She looked up from the kitchen doorway to see shimmers calling out the firmament's essence in a silent way. Ardent city expressions of the good life had fallen on deaf ears a long time ago. But, the new home called Tareni was an invocation to memory, finally. The long days and the emptiness of night time drove in many messages for the tired consciousness, inarticulate feeling, impassive distance. Ravi closed the rooms and walked up to her small study desk. There lay a final reversal, among many unexpected twists and turns, that would, finally, decide Razi's future.

***

Chapter 5

ab uno disce omnes

The rains were a welcome reprieve from everything that had gone before. Razi sat on her large wicker chair, thinking about and planning her first lunch party. She was, as yet, uncertain about friends and familiarity in Tareni but the freedom of her new home was irridescent, overriding, easing. The people of Tareni, by and large, were unknown to Razi with just a few emerging into her life in unobtrusive ways. The air was tense somehow in the city centres but she was careful not to allow this to be a deterrence, another abstraction, repetitive discrimination. She did not delve into her life's early years as many in her circles did nor rush into the future as a lesson from the past. Now, she had given herself this final restitution which would restore, for her, the world's inundating deficiencies. The well-educated veneer presented by many in society was often tattered and worn out by brutal upswings in the public consciousness. Territorialism was not abided by in any sphere but had run rampant within the offices. Commercialists by definition, leaders from the business sectors would revert to simpler arrangements, wiping many slates clean without any deliberate memoranda. Razi often thought of herself as a hapless broker in this large dimension. The plainness of her morning, today, unleashed a subconscious correction of chaos and perpetuity. She stood up from the chair and planned to visit the arcades once again. The new city offered many unchanneled rediscoveries but, alone, she was determined to set her own course and social identity. Women in the city did not rise up against chauvinism any longer but chose to remedy the material deficits that had resulted from aggressive power.

"Good morning!" The voice was loud and raspy. Razi looked up from her shop display to see a tall man with spectacles, watching her in a peculiar way. "Good morning," She replied without any hesitation. As she sat for a cup of tea at the restaurant close by, she looked around to see who else was there. A few city locals were busy talking among themselves as though she, too, ought to be doing the same. She sipped the tea which tasted flat and insipid. The man who had greeted her walked into the restaurant and, in the same motion, walked out from a smaller door near the road. Razi sat trying to remember if she had said anything untoward because a similar scene had recurred over many years in her city. She looked at the teapot carelessly placed on the table and sat silently for a while. An indescribable anxiety had regressed yet she knew that the troubles of the past would require a firm hand. Tareni would not be wrested from anyone or herself. Halse was adamant about his placements and she would, alternately, have to resolve freedom and autonomy in less precarious ways. The sudden collusion of disparate thoughts on

CHAPTER 5

unequalled problems made Razi visibly uncomfortable and she left the restaurant feeling alone. On the way back home, there were whizzing cars along the road that swerved in a different sort of way. She walked slowly at first, watching the road's edge with an intense focus. An unfortunate, factual, festering misidentification of people and places was evident but without any lethal affect posed by the city.

Razi reached her clustered neighbourhood in short, measured, uncharacteristic steps. She stopped near a red brick fence and saw a man waving at a bus that had just driven away into the distance. "Do you have a car?" He rasped out at Razi who stood a few steps away. She stood frozen and frightened for some time and did not answer his question. The skies had clouded again and the neighbourhood was empty despite the inviting homes bunched together in a triangular arc. The lean and sallow man was not young nor pleasant yet his seething countenance seemed all too common. His shoes were sharp and pointed while his clothing resembled a dramatic resumption of theatricality itself. He waited for Razi to reply and leaned on the brick fence with a contemptuous smile. Reza remembered this exact encounter from years ago in and around the city. The residents would often rush out with their dogs and walk around in a severe march. Just the year before, she had stood under a small tree and argued vehemently with another disturbed person for an hour. Following this incident, Halse planted thin bamboo stalks around the gates as a protective measure. The man, today, was ready for an argument and sneered at the homes in the vicinity. "No, I don't own a car." She replied finally and looked at the man in a stunned way. "Well, I am already late for my meeting. This place has no sense of time or even a good taxi service. You live here?" He said in a hoarse tone and took out a wallet that was made of dark, untanned leather. "The bus stop is nearby. You have to walk only a few blocks to get to it. This is a private neighbourhood." Razi spoke in a measured and slow tone, watching the man's jerky movements and waiting for a violent reaction.

***

The dark wooden door seemed like a cruel insertion on Razi's new home as she walked in and shut it behind herself. She bolted the latch and walked into the dining room. Looking at the clock quickly, she drank a glass of water and sat for a few minutes. There was no news of violent clashes anywhere in Tareni or the city. Yet, her chance meeting with the sneering man reminded her of all the incidents and encounters now being investigated in precise detail. The windows in her home were small and shiny but the fresh breeze gushed in as temporary salvation. Taking off her shoes, she looked at her feet for signs of bruises and calluses. There were none. Her hands, too, looked unblemished by the sun and the dusty distancing. Her beautiful handbag on the dining table singed many anxieties now, strangely, in the foreground. It was not a simple life that had lost or won, but, a bestial attitude that loomed large, often, and hid in the shadows when the tide began to turn. The city's enforced segregations and quickly derived motives had worked, worn down a sinister history, wasted no thought. Women and children could be seen playing in the makeshift parks while the unequated notion of the foreign would weave certainty and awareness into everyone's conversations. Had she lost a position of strength or just the comforts of habit? She thought about her professional growth in the city but, today, the jaded and ulterior devolutions were foreshadowed by Tareni. They would have to stop, cede to order, derive no more than their own mindlessness. She opened a book from the bookcase and flipped through it. *"It was that combined silence and sound, of the statue of the commander, but this stony step had something indescribably enormous and multiple about it which awakened the idea of a throng, and, at the same time, the idea of a spectre. "* Les Misérables was not one of her favourite books but the passage brought tears to her eyes.

The next day was an uncrafted delay of plans and fulfillments. Razi woke up early and sorted out yet another collection of daily necessities. As she placed her belongings in neat, well-spaced corners and compartments, she began to think of her working life as a crescendo of both inertia and determined energy. The office people she had worked with over the years would often comment on these extreme oppositions in their own lives too. Yet, for Razi, there was no alternative until now, until saturation had become inevitable. She thought to herself with deep introspection as if a culmination was imminent and ending. Had she broken the ethic or rested it in a quiet place? Business deliberations in the city were, mostly, closed by legal instrumentation and severe restrictions which were workable premises until her move to Tareni. The sudden opening of a distant terrain of people and linearity had caused a shift for Razi, invoking a sensory present, an arc of necessary change, a disorganising future. She finished settling her clothes and walked down into the small garden that, today, stood alone yet fortressed by lush vegetation. While walking around the lawn, she heard sounds of the ground being beaten in measured thumps. The neighbours had left for work and the relentless sounds seared into the calm neighbourhood in an uncanny message of abatement. She stood on top of a small stone in the garden and peeped outside the fence. A group of men were stacking firewood in a space near the perimeter with furtive precision. She could not see their faces properly but the moment was a memory undone rather than a new encounter or incursion. She watched them finish their work and walk into the main road in a line. "It's just firewood, not an infernal blaze." Appearing behind them, the sallow man from yesterday said sneeringly and followed the men into the road without any warning.

Late in the afternoon, Razi checked her kitchen cupboard and wrote a few shopping reminders for the new week. She latched the front door and walked outside towards the provision stores at the end of the road. The clouded skies had opened up with unwavering brightness and the place appeared flooded by sunlight. Ahead of the road lay large and empty plots of land that greened during the monsoons and turned dour as winter made a chilling start. She looked around for a few minutes and wondered whether she would acclimatise well enough. Her new neighbourhood was not the cluster she was used to nor a well-worn city suburb. A large electricity pole near the provision store was being repaired and she stopped to look at the clumped wires. "The town hall is well-lit but not anywhere else." An eerily familiar voice disrupted her silent walk and she looked at the man from the neighbourhood talking to a farmer who was carrying his carts to the stores. The farmer was distinctly recognizable but the man beside him was, still, a menacing presence. Razi walked up to the store and said, "I'll be needing fresh vegetables and bread too. The meat store is nearby, isn't it?" The shopkeeper was about to reply when the tall man interrupted, saying, "The fallow seasons will show stagnant life, once and for all."

***

Chapter 6

audere est facere

"It is a deeply held belief here that the evening signifies rest and a good passage of time, Razi. I am comfortable here because of these values and ideals. I would have been miserable elsewhere." Devi said in a lilting tone as they conversed over the telephone. Razi stopped for a few seconds, slightly shocked at this revelation. 'That's good to know, Devi. I was anxious about this change of place but the journey was very motivating and this home is just what I need. Are there any political issues here still making the rounds in the suburbs? I still laugh at that joke about dusty files piling up in the courthouses. We did not delve too much into these bureaucratic problems earlier." She replied in a short breath, humoured by Devi and apprehensive about what lay ahead at the same time. The line was silent for a few more seconds and Devi replied, "But, as always, Razi, the authoritarian lot always reserves judgment while other hostile parties come here with scars from elsewhere. Has there ever been any real and lasting solution for this mela, really?" Devi chuckled as she recounted a perpetual, prevaricating, indoctrinated state that had inserted itself into Nepali life. Razi laughed along with her and, soon, it was clear that both women had sought to subvert this crude perpetuity over the years but without much success. "Well, I don't know about scars or solutions but why don't we meet for lunch on Saturday at my new home? It'll be just us and my new friends. I spoke with Halse and he seems to see a light at the end of the tunnel." The day had shown its resolve and disputation unequivocally, especially for Razi and her cousin. "That is our solution, Razi. I'll bring some dessert." Devi's answer stayed with Razi as a summary warning and guidance for many years.

The conversation with Devi pulled open many wishes and hopes that Razi had agonised over, in the past. She was given to worrying over the static nature of her immediate friendships in the city. Tareni could, however, be a chance to share better sociability, an unconditioned community, a spirited group. The years were not dragging on nor disappearing into high-paced work systems as they had in the past decade. But, it was also a tide that had swept away city angst, too. Her neighbour was feeding the sparrows next door and she stepped outside to talk with her. "I was wondering if you'd be free to come over for lunch soon. My cousin thinks we are all in need of good gatherings." Razi said immediately and saw a beaming smile appear on her neighbour. "Thank you, Razi. I feed the sparrows sometimes as though they were my only companions. Lunch would be lovely." Shreela replied and pointed to the small bowl of bird seeds. "They are very faithful, though. I shouldn't complain." They laughed at the irony withheld by a world that provided without hesitation and, yet, delineated no signs of contentment or happiness. The informality of everyday strictures was a keenly felt imposition in many places in Nepal. Women would give up their social lives and turn to spiritual assemblages in sheer numbers. The superstitions associated with changed living were, however, invisible or understated. The smaller towns and cities were beset by misplaced interpretations of the virtuous presence, identifiability, a deserving upliftment. Through their conversation, Razi noticed in her neighbour a kinship that was not inherited nor surrounded by sundry ties among and between places. The people in her new city were ardently individual, collectivised, cautious by conventionality. "We will have a nice get-together and enjoy betterment right here in Tareni, then." Smiling and relieved, the two women entered their homes with the shared relation of a present that ought to have been reclaimed many years ago.

A circumference of eventualities and slacken undoings were at the back of Razi's mind the next day. Somehow, a new area had brought about many unexpected revisions in her life and in her way of doing things. It had been a slew of rushed decisions on Halse and her part to ensure their move away from the city was successful although the attendant details now seemed far too prompted. Their lives in the city were comfortably urban but Tareni had evoked the subconscious life in a grim yet pragmatic enough manner. Sitting in her bedroom, Razi watched the area unfold outside her window while her thoughts began to shape in new directions. The districts were restructuring administration itself while people were starting to step out of a furious silence, an unwelcomed sway, unbeholden rancour. "I hope you remember me from our journey together here. I'm Razi and we met in town a few days back." Razi said in a clear voice to her travel companion over the telephone. "Of course! How are you, Razi? It is nice to hear from you. I thought it was a call from out of town for a second." Razi's new friend replied in a brief moment that reversed many nagging misgivings about everyday company for both women. "I'm settling in here and I hope you are too. The place is so different but so familiar, isn't it?" Razi said in a personable voice that she reserved only for her family and close friends. "Yes, my thoughts exactly," came the hurried reply. After a lengthy discussion spanning exactly the travel moments each had encountered, Razi said, "Please come for lunch at my new place on Saturday. It's just by the outer road bend. We can enjoy an afternoon away from crowded problems." Her new friend chuckled but replied in an emotional tone after a pause, "That would be super. I was caught up in my unsettled dailies, too." Razi's quick-thinking plan for introductions within her new community had reawoken many clustered wishes, anxious meanings, forgone indecisions.

***

"The roast is perfect, Razi. I am blessed with relatives like you." Devi said as she chose a piece of roast chicken from the platter with a swirl of a large spoon. Razi had brought some of her mother's silver serving spoons and washed them carefully for the lunch gathering. They sparkled as her guests heaped the delicious Nepali fare onto their plates. "Necessity brings out the best in some of us, doesn't it? My cousin here was a force to be reckoned with when we were young. The world was going to surge ahead and pack away the past in an advancing movement, according to Razi. Now, we are enjoying roast with this wonderful cutlery, lost to many cultural divides." The four women laughed loudly and ate in spoonfuls of enjoyment. "The country cannot afford people to be at a loss because of new-fangled ideas which do not apply well here. The other day, I was told that my program experience would see other valuations but that I should not lose heart. I told them, finally, that my daily work would not be stalled by ignorant novelties." Razi and her companions were discussing the waves of transformation that had spouted new territorialities and, concomitantly, thrown up every concealed and sinister problem in the city systems. "It is time, again, to assert our value system and our self-interests. The good intentions of the past are reaching a dead end without anything but apathy." Shreela was a teacher and university administrator who had always held the belief that progressive ideals in Nepal would see fruition only through mass reach. "That's true but our hands are tied. We have lost our connection to the common good in terrible ways. Perhaps, the syndrome is not external but, in fact, a stagnation of our lives and not the stagnant economy they write about." Razi said, looking at her guests thoughtfully as they listened with brightening expressions.

"There are many elements in society who forget where we hail from. My early remembrance of blockades and political protest seems like a tale of misled zeal now. Men in the city perimeter here watch and wait for shadows instead of buses and birds." Shreela said calmly as the lunch gathering divulged hilarious counterpoints to intrusion and upward mobility in their lives. Razi stood up shaking her head and closed the window which had begun to move with the strong breeze from the west. "I worry that we might lose our peace of mind to fanciful notions of democracy in the wrong arenas." She said and sat down on a high cushion. The public realm in Tareni was deft and undaunted but many women had reeled from a sinister segregation of home life occurring, haphazardly, in spates of recognizable malignancy. The day had morphed into a gathering of dispersed living and one that would reform many calculated misalignments. "There was a man nearby, a few days back, who asked me, in a mean tone, if I owned a car. I remember being asked this exact question so many times. It's always a mean insinuation, though." Razi said in a light-hearted tone but her guests watched her in a sudden silence. "Serious motivations should not be taken lightly anywhere. Tell me when you are going into the city and I'll join you." Shreela said after a few minutes. "No, no. I was returning home then. He sounded like he was counting status symbols." Razi's reply made the rest laugh uncontrollably and the discussion soon veered into an easy conviviality. "So, they will continue the town hall meetings despite recurring blockages? I was keen to see our city office see through on the new plans." Devi's pointed question relegated the ungainly neighbourhood disturbances back to their rightful place. "The day will come when Tareni's aspirations for the upcoming memoranda reach the correct office." Shaili, Razi's travel friend, said as she cleared the table and stacked the plates and dishes carefully yet unthinkingly.

Evening set in without any taut or tangent reminder. Razi's

lunch gathering had established bonds and earmarked forgotten articulations on empowerment, insolvent pressures, women's disappearing prerogatives. Rightful paths and approaches were set up, on occasion, as social and economic directions steered away from communities yet many stratified apprehensions and doubts remained indelible within the home and at work. Commercial proliferation was not as harmful as in other nations while the merit class had undone much of the inchoate political upsurge of the past decades. Razi finished cleaning up and switched on the lights with a sigh of relief. Was a sense of belonging inculcated through living cultures rather than as an actual understanding of one's place in the nation? Vehement declarations of powerful ideology were symbolic in everyday life as both political and deterministic. Unquestioned and shifted, the answers resided in many communities for whom there were other pressing daily matters to tide over. The next day, Razi woke up early and set out for the city centre in a determined move forward. The arcade she had visited was opening in small steps of insightful details. She walked into an arched corridor-like row of buildings near the arcade and studied the wares carefully. "It must be eleven o'clock. There are too many people here already." The loudly garbled voice pierced through the crowd in a flash of a second. People shopping and working on and around the street looked at this man in absolute unison. Seconds passed and, as though an event was over, many of them, including Razi, walked into the outer perimeter. As she reached the end of the street, Razi turned around to see the man sitting hunched near a large window. It seemed as though he was defending himself in an arena filled with people who had decided to attack the offence in a quick reprisal.

CHAPTER 6

***

Chapter 7

aurea mediocritas

The small stone shrine at the farthest edge of the foothill was bathed in fulsome sunshine as Razi walked along the small gravel road. The morning walk was a tradition in her family that had seen many ups and downs of political history and disenchantment. Her mother often coached Razi and her relatives when she was a young child and referred to it as a trip to the enchanted forest. She remembered her family in a sombre moment as the stone shone with chromatic intensity. Droplets of water scattered themselves around the shrine in an elemental premise, a spiritual obeisance, the natural transcendence. Watching this devotional, Razi felt an awareness of her own life emerge out of a shadowed past. Was she now destined to forge a new life or transfer it towards Tareni and some semblance of freedom? The shrine looked like an ancient parable with small spots of vermillion carefully dotted around it. Razi's family history was an extensive one, with her forebears having worked in many places of import yet their memory was tinged with bitterness and an uneasy compromise. She had lived most of her working life applying methods and practices that made easy answers possible and true in the strictest sense. Discursive dialogues in the city were primarily geared towards popular disenchantments which smarted of inconclusivity. The shrine had always held a special place in Razi's family and, today, she felt the presence of a higher order with a sharp twinge. City dwellers did not forget their religious traditions, for the most part, although it was evident that many people had lost faith in their spiritual canons. The morning was beginning to emanate from a dim dawn with a perceptively different air than Razi was used to. Perhaps, she thought to herself, there was a way to live a chosen path and agency.

On the way home, she stopped near a clump of trees and watched sparrows splatter around in a large puddle of water. The water was clear and stony while the birds danced around in it with glee. Walking into her neighbourhood, she looked at the buildings with a renewed sense of awareness. The houses were nearly hidden and shaded by greenery and trees but the brick designs were a strong presence, an artery of comfort, a traditional overture. Smiling to herself, she went into the living room and sat with a glass of fresh juice. The sparrows, too, were an old family lore and her mother would sometimes fill bird seeds on a planter to see if they would stay or return to the hills. The years had passed without warning in the city for Razi and family gatherings would, usually, turn into wintertime occasions. Halse was a gracious family man yet there were times when Razi saw through the easy conversations and dinner table humouring. The city had chosen its methods too. After a while, she sifted through a box filled with her work papers. The printed photocopies and browning files were staple reminders for city dwellers. Today, she read through the filed bills and envelopes with a mixture of annoyance and laughter. The meticulously organized papers and office records had assumed a tenuous place in Razi's life and there was little collusion left within the work system which the records could hide or, indeed, expose. Was an overhaul imminent in the nation's flailing economic environment or just an anticipated breakdown, she thought to herself. Signs pointed in the opposite direction but these inked and signed remnants of her work had jogged Razi's memory just as much as the morning walk. It was a curative time to revise her own preoccupation with professional targets.

Shreela and Razi met the next day and talked with each other for close to an hour. It was as though the two were closely tied by their neighbourhood but also through a convergence of untimely flux in their cities. "A town lifestyle suits us, Razi. We were all coached for professional success and we achieve it, for the most part. But, we are who we are and the birds know it too." Shreela said in a moment of introspection. The front lawn in her house was well-cared for and green. The small and comfortable chairs near the front door allowed the breeze to sway in and out. Razi looked at Shreela for a while before replying. "I cannot agree more but I am from the city. Maybe, it will pan out in its course. Work is centred there and I have many good years ahead still." The two women were no strangers to upheaval and struggle but years of experience in managing daily work showed in their tough stance. They watched the day's sunlit aura in the garden guide them towards a peacability that was rare during workdays.

CHAPTER 7

"My husband's contact in the *Nagarpalika* thinks we are in the midst of a small revolution. You must join me for a meeting there soon, They set the system straight for many people." Shreela said in a single breath and held out some cookies on a plate. Razi was taken aback by this divulgence and waited before she replied. "The meetings there are a far cry from the usual office board rooms." Shreela was adamant in an innocuous sort of way as Razi smiled and said, "I will certainly see if I fit into the meeting agenda." The neighbourhood was a truism as it had never been before for both of them. The shaded edges had eked out an air of communal reformation that was visible, venal. etymological.

"But, Halse, there are wonderful people everywhere." Razi cut short Halse's long narrative on his days with exacting optimism. There was silence over the telephone and she heard him cough. "There are? Well, I'll be starting my own search too. The embargo was a myth and now you have trailed into a social group. I can see good fortune for us up ahead!" He exclaimed and listened to his wife laugh through to the end of the conversation. Their spheres of influence and affluence were not expansive nor heavily societal but the seeds of necessity had, finally, sprung into new life. "The definitions here are not troublesome. I might even join Shreela for a meeting at the *Nagapalika*. New political stresses face newer dissolutions too. My lunch was a nice gathering. Devi remembers our silverware!" Razi said while they discussed their immediate plans.

A shared past had reverberated in many places in the past months while radical change was predicted, reduced, inverted into shape. In the hinterlands, the rough and tumble of daily work would not run a paltry course for much longer and Razi had seen, first-hand, how strife was unprocessed and blockaded in Tareni. The stone shrine was still a mystical articulation but its profound nature had strengthened passages into the destined much as it was known to in historical accounts. Globalised cultures had revived a few well-known standards in the city as had international cooperation. The messaged catalysing of progressive norms and practicalities, however, was far too endemic for lightweight shifts. Razi wandered around her new home for the rest of the day mulling over the work re-alignments that lay ahead. Was an emergence the final hurdle, she thought to herself. The comfort of her new home and her friends in Tareni appeared as simple changes but the inversions into a changed order were becoming intensely conscious, advertent, the past's providence.

***

"Enmity is inculcated these days. It used to be a warrior's shield, they say." Devi exclaimed in an intense tone when Razi handed her a file of papers. "Please keep these for me until Halse comes home. They are my work agreements from the city. You must not let enmity or even the idea of enemies overtake your life. It takes all kinds to make this world, as they say." Razi replied in a matter-of-fact tone while Devi looked at her with a shocked expression. "It's just for safekeeping, Devi. You look troubled." She said again but Devi did not reply for a while and the late afternoon hid much of the rest of the day in a bright haze. "You were planning to get back to work." Devi's voice seemed shaken but Razi replied, "I will but I'll take some time

CHAPTER 7

away as I had planned." Rays of sunshine whispered into the room in playful lines. "Well, that's my worry. People must not feel pressured because of their professions. It is time for the administration systems to recognise this vital fact." The strong-willed nature of people in Tareni came through as Devi recounted her worries. In consonance, the darkened humility of persistently ulterior forces inimical to the hinterlands was beginning to swarm towards a counterpoint. "Was there a lot of backstabbing in the city while you were working there?" Devi asked Razi quietly and simply. Razi thought of an answer for a while and said, "It's a city, Devi. The broad span of different types of people and difference itself create friction. I managed well." The words were deafening to hear even for Devi who was part and parcel of the work systems in the two cities. In a moment's flash, Devi looked at Razi and smiled a beaming smile as if she had understood the gambit too. "We'll enjoy lunch at the arcade soon. This is not a time for gloomy memories." With that, the two ladies moved back into their homes and decided to shift the problematized past into a lesser burden, an untenuous faultline, a homily. Razi cleaned the house with a scarf wrapped around her hair and was, soon, cooking her favourite bowl of rice and curry in swift motion. The memory of her youth was a new remembrance. She sat at the table and enjoyed her meal while the evening slid into a starlit sky. It was rare for her to spend time in introspection yet the calming influence of an evening's silence brought with it time for thought and reappraisals.

The days flowed from one to another in a temporality that was new to Razi. She spent most of her days in her home, often resting during the day and watching the dusk emblazon a colourful course on Tareni. The mornings would spring up on the residents as though this small built environment was owed a small cessation of daily disruptions and intrusion. "Did you find what you were looking for?" said a gruff voice as Razi walked into the green field that was hidden behind her home area. She looked around and saw an elderly woman, carrying a wicker basket on her back filled with oranges. Razi smiled immediately at the lady. shook her head and replied, "I'm just discovering Tareni's many hidden places." The elderly woman clicked her tongue and walked away as though their brief encounter had been in vain. Razi stood watching her walk into the edge of the field wondering if people in Tareni knew her move to the neighbourhood. Realising that she had been accosted in similar ways many times, she sat under a large tree and looked around. The late afternoon was usually hectic in the office and city but this slowed pace of life struck Razi as almost hallucinatory, halting, a healed space. Walking back home, she remembered the man she had run into and decided to change the lamp lights quickly. Shreela's house gate was latched but the lush garden was a welcome sight. Had the new city returned to her a forgotten threshold, she thought and opened her front door. The house appeared still but welcoming and she looked at the large windows for a second. Halse's deft refurbishments in their city home would cause a stir in the community because of the unexpected colours and modern touches he added. Her new space was a cleaving departure, the singular, indeterminate. Taking out new lamps from a box, she wiped them with a washcloth and replaced the old ones. With each new lamp in its correct stand, she switched on the lights and saw a brightening effect sweep her home. This was not the clandestine change Razi had believed it to be nor any uncharted lessening of life.

"Do you think another uprising will happen? I mean there's been so much talk of interims and orders even from official quarters." Razi asked her travel friend in a moment of openness and candour. Her friend sat watching the faraway hills and attempted to reply in earnest. "The cities are not places for revolution, Razi. It's the law being manipulated elsewhere, that's all. People will rise up and remove the criminality but it should not be part of everyday life." She said after a few minutes with an air of resignation. "Well, if the reports are to be believed, justice is within reach, too," Razi said with a firm expression and bought her usual stack of bread and biscuits. Her friend watched her and began to smile and laugh at the same time. "It's not a time for rations and supply politics again, is it?" Razi looked at her in an impish way and the two resumed their conversation along the city's suburban road in a different sort of mood. It was a standard that had been wrested, violated and tainted. It would be yet another standard that would be curative, instilled, an ingrained virtue for all to see. "I'll be joining my family soon in the highlands. We could make a trip to Khumbu too." She said with a smile and cemented a bond that was long overdue. Razi went back home, laughing to herself and remembering her childhood with young highland children who would weave small baskets for her and her cousins to play with. The dialogue on continuity and broken ties had seen many intellectual analyses but the communal systems were not easily swayed nor repaired. The air was fresh and balmy in the neighbourhood. Would there, in fact, be more political insolvency for the cities to contend with, Razi thought to herself. Her suitcases were neatly stacked in the store area and she thought about her trip to Tareni as fortuitous now. The emptiness of the streets itself was a comfort and a blessing in disguise. As she switched the television on, she forgot about her fixations with the news and views of the world. The television droned on without much by way of sensational deliberations. The substance of life in Nepali cities and towns had somehow trodden into less mania, lesser decibels, lessened vitriol.

***

Chapter 8

humilitas occidit superbiam

"Good morning, friends and colleagues." The *Nagarpalika* liaison said in a clear and concise tone. Razi, Shreela and Devi were sitting in a large rectangular office close to the front entrance. The chairs were lined around and a few desks were pushed towards the windows. Razi wore a wind sheeter jacket that she had bought in the city and looked apprehensive until this greeting. She smiled at the liaison and settled into an unofficial and impromptu meeting that would pave the way for her and many women in Tareni. The office room was spacious and empty aside from the chairs and desks. A lined arrangement was becoming the norm in many work agendas but, today, it was more than just another group coming together to discuss important daily affairs. "Let me start with this quote," the meeting facilitator said. "Necessity is blind until it becomes conscious. Freedom is the consciousness of necessity. The words are from Karl Marx and we will consider these words important for their meaning and impact." His words reverberated around the meeting room and the participants appeared serious yet involved. The liaison was a government veteran who had worked in Tareni for many years. He hailed from the neighbouring town and had travelled to the West many times for study purposes. Of a similar age to Razi and her companions, he was known to be firm and polite in every community agenda. The collective mood in the room had changed from one of cautious consideration to one of a restrained purpose, an issued semiology, a proud clarity. "Tareni is my home too and I believe we can solve many problems together." He said again and watched the rest turn thoughtful and introspective. The agenda for the day was simple but the people bore signs of far too many improbabilities for it to be a mere work day event. Razi was silent but her companions could see that this was an unchallenged arena for her and many others. "We have new administrations reverting old systems for better applications here now. A major breakthrough, in my mind." He said finally and sat near the desk. The empty desks and a table in the far corner stood, wooden and impassive, as a message from everyone and no one.

The meeting surged forward with many well-worn and new points of departure being tabled and explained in minute detail. "We are a realistic administration, Dai. You must remember that the floodgates are not for us. We simply bide our time when fallout is the norm." A young Nagarpalika officer said in the middle of the conversations. The room became silent and tense. Razi was watching and listening intently, shocked sometimes and eager not to miss a single sentence. Shreela nudged her and said, "Is this alright for you? I've already told Dai that you are here from the city and you are a hardworking professional." Razi nodded and chuckled at the same time. The men in the room were mostly from Tareni from the office districts while the women were from neighbouring settlements too. "I can relate to much of what they are saying. But I had better not say much and listen instead." Razi replied and saw Shreela and Devi smile in an uncharacteristic moment. The meeting was being transcribed by a young man who looked at Razi often while doing his work. She had never participated in a town hall such as this and could not hide her interest. "Commercialism is not the problem per se. It is the exploitative nature of systemic proliferation that causes people to seek out their own disorders. The time is ripe for a thorough reassessment." A man wearing a sports jacket said after a while and waited for the rest to respond to his provocation. There was silence for a few minutes while the *Nagarpalika* guards walked in and stood near the door. They left within a few minutes and the room was soon buzzing with discussions. "Education here leans towards discipline, Dai. Those injustices must not take away from an established university system." The liaison stood up and walked near the window. "A subversion of failed intentions cannot sink us anymore. The winds of change will favour us someday soon." Razi had not expected Tareni to offer her a momentous conclave such as this and she sat watching another world unfold before her eyes. This world was pragmatic, placed in wise belief, unprevalent. It was, vitally, an order for living.

"Appropriation is an unkind phenomenon, certainly. But, we are gearing up for a better ethic." With this statement, the discussions veered towards principles of daily existence and away from a phenomenology that had struck hard in Tareni and the towns that were closed away from the capital city. Razi heard his words and felt an immeasurable alienation ease away from her mind. She was not given to debating politics with her family nor her immediate circles but the town hall was a definite shift and an articulation long overdue for many working women. There was a quick burst of laughter as the young officer moved the desks into the corner and placed more chairs in the emptied space. Devi smiled at Razi and Shreela and said, "That's for us to understand. Tough times call for more chairs and space!" The three women giggled in bursts of laughter as the rest watched them with a knowing smile. The meeting had evolved into an agenda without any forewarning. But, the convenor knew that the goal in the far distance was within reach. Interior dialogues were rare in Tareni and other towns but Razi's presence had sparked an unapproached element in the community. "Transformations will occur. It is but natural but we must not wield the angry mentality into our daily duties." Razi and her companions looked up at the *Nagapalika* liaison in a serious way, remembering their anxiety over many public disruptions and resulting encounters with aggression. "Dai, we are mere residents in this rising tide. Our working lives bear the brunt only to a certain extent." Shreela said in a grave tone which purported to hide her apprehensions but exposed all underlying fallacies instead. The liaison did not reply and looked around the room, seeing only similar expressions of hateful disrepair, an unwilling recognition, the silenced logic. He waited for the rest to take up the conversation and, very soon, people in the room were talking with each other, without reservation, about the hidden truths that stamped their everyday burdens.

CHAPTER 8

***

"Human values reconcile not only differences but also the past and the present, Shreela. It's a necessary rite for us to leave our woes behind and re-align with the essential." Razi said as they walked towards their neighbourhood. "I wish we weren't always rushing about trying to resolve the past and our lives in the here and now." "Yes, but our nature and needs show this in a stark way. We have to move ahead not break away." Shreela replied with a stern expression. These rare moments of insight and unblighted camaraderie had reappeared in Tareni through fundamentally altered circumstances. The two walked in a pensive mood, trying to understand the meeting's proceedings in their entirety. "It's almost a new world for me to be in a town hall meeting in Tareni," Razi replied with a sudden sway of her head. She turned to see if there was anyone behind them and proceeded to her gate. Shreela stood and watched the road bend into a gravel path in the farthest corner. They were experiencing an overwhelming feeling of relief but the doctrines were not rooted in mere political reason. It was as though a new future was within their grasp and, together, they would have to forge it in good faith. Many empowered women throughout Nepali history had sought an alternative autonomy with resounding success. Was there, indeed, a similar fate for them, Razi thought as she closed the gate. Devi had gone home too and was sitting in her patio reading the newspaper. Work gatherings were plentiful in their communities but there were far too many untested and trivial ways to contend with and defuse. The day had crossed over into a moment in history while evening saw to it that there was unison, woven space, hopeful decisions. Smoothing out her tablecloth, Razi sat and prepared her dinner in a serene atmosphere. The tinted blue skies had not lost their promise nor a halo of calm. She thought about calling Halse over the telephone but decided to wait till the next day. The darkening surroundings did not seem ominous as in the past and she switched on the television. Would she join a movement with the town hall people, she thought as the news media deepened an ongoing retrospection. Halse was sure to decipher important statements in the meeting's proceedings. For Razi, the uncoded years were behind her and she was certain to unbind the despairing and ungainly problems accruing from another era. It was a decided solidarity that was imminent and the impounded notions of fair play had seared into the public imagination. Complicated failures in the public systems had seeped into everyday trials. The gradual undoing of signified and identifiable livelihood values had met its final customary.

"It is the flow of capital that has been co-opted, Razi. Accessibility was quietly revamped in Nepal many times throughout history. They should check the annals for ideas on how to forge ties that will not exploit a fair and equal system." Shreela said as Razi and she stood outside the kitchen doors and talked with each other over the small iron gate. Taken aback by this candid revelation, Razi nodded and tried to think of something to say. "We have become used to making ends meet. Maybe this time there will be a viable solution from the people." She said again in an unsmiling way and appeared equally surprised by her own words. "Yes. I lean towards ideas of collective bargaining but, I think, this has run its course too. There is a need for strength and numbers all around." Razi replied after a long pause with a peculiar smile. The two were still thinking through the town hall meeting in their minds and were struck by the ideas that had emerged in it. "Well, my time away from work will not be in vain," Razi said again with a determined look and waved out as Shreela left for work. Was there, indeed, a vault from the past to help understand and recalibrate a time of changing promisories, Razi thought and returned to her room. Sitting at her desk, she opened her large file holder and reread some of the printed pages in it. The radical belief in cooperation was not tested by questions of morality as much as by those of ethics. She underlined a few sentences with her pen, unwilling, for an instance, to allow any faulty or fallible clause to damage her reading. It is rooted in pragmatism, then, she thought to herself as she closed the file and looked outside from the window. Sunlit greenery shook in the light breeze creating a fluidity which she had found beguiling as a young child. Were the large floral plants swaying or shaking with laughter, she wondered with a lightened mind while the day wandered into a balmy equation.

"Lawlessness is a cruel symptom, Razi. Many societies suffer the consequences but, in equal parts, find the precise measures that must be wrought or, even, etched in stone." Halse said in a short breath, eager to discuss their days and time alone. "You worry a lot. I can understand that but it takes a while for our issues to find the right steps, too. Don't take too much to heart." He said again as Razi burst into laughter. "Here, we have our supper in a canteen and it is the best thing to have happened to us all. We've found the time and the groups to sit and reminisce about our lives over a glass of mulled wine. Imagine!" With that, Halse had set the tone and pace for Razi's time in Tareni. "Yes, dear! We hear many stories but the real stories are yet to find good endings." Razi said humorously but the telephone was silent for a few minutes. Halse had been given a brief account of the town hall meeting by Razi and, now, he found yet another unarticulated plight being solved by Razi's quick-thinking attitude. "I will wait and see how you fare with the new administrative people. The workers' movement is not a new phenomenon in the world." He said cautiously as the two found themselves rethinking everything from local movements to the corrosion of broad-spectrum change itself. Razi sat on her bed and looked at her room after the telephone call. Her room was comfortable but uninviting even to herself. Taking the large chair from one corner towards the window, she rearranged the furniture and decided to buy some house plants the next time she visited the big arcade in town. The new carpet on the floor was a welcome reprieve and she sat at her desk, once again, opening a box that contained her jewellery and other belongings. A small diamond brooch shone with the sun's rays as she looked at her belongings with a sense of comfort. The city did not spare time for fanciful notions of ownership and pride but it did unfurl towards a living, breathing, unacculturated sphere of personhood. There were times when Razi felt the need to lock away her life through small elements of her possessions. And, yet, Tareni had opened up to her with uncharacterized norms that were beneficent, an undoing of wrongs, history's everyday translatability. After dinner, she walked to the gate and closed the lock carefully. As she switched the lights off around the living room, the carpet under her feet felt soft and luscious. The sofa is a blessing, she thought to herself and walked up to her bedroom in near darkness.

CHAPTER 8

***

Chapter 9

montani semper liberi

"My father used to call me Raina because I liked to play in the rain. I even forgot my real name for a while in school in Khumbu where he worked." Razi's travel friend, Shaili, said with a peal of laughter remembering her childhood. "The big electricity plant was a fundamental problem for them because the government would curse them for causing modern troubles. They would sit and watch the river as if it was a sacred formation." Razi laughed too as she listened to her friend recount her life in the upstream areas that were now considered a journey too far. "I did travel up to the mountain villages when I was young but I don't remember much," Razi replied quietly remembering her family's strict disapproval of people's interest in the mountainous regions. The shallow reformations for equity and safe development had run their course and eroded as an unworthy political destiny. People and places, however, stamped out interference and scarcity with undeterred might. "Where do you think modernity will take us all, Shaili? There is always a need for objectivity but bad development takes its toll quite blatantly." Razi asked in a quiet moment while Shaili attempted to steer the conversation away from the accursed nature of power politics. "The town hall meeting was such an important one for me. Doctrines do not spare anyone." Shaili watched her friend for a while and looked around the arcade with a tinge of bitterness. The two walked around the complex and window-shopped for almost an hour before entering a restaurant. "Halse would be writing notes if he were here. He thinks the pursuits of the intellectual will save our country." Shaili sat at a table near the centre of the restaurant and pointed towards the shelves at the back. There were stacks of homemade aperitifs, branded and reasonably priced, which made everyone in the restaurant feel consciously at home. "I'll have a nice old-fashioned cup of tea today," Razi said to the waitress who looked pleased to see the two women appreciate their new hideout. "I could tell you stories about modern dilemmas but even those are a little dented and rusty," Shaili replied and ordered her mid-afternoon coffee.

"Was the wage issue in the city dealt with by a firm hand?" Shaili asked suddenly as they walked out of the restaurant. Razi replied in a strangely rough voice, "The city administration knows mathematics well." She looked ahead and saw the man from her neighbourhood encounter move around towards the arcade facade a few times and walk back into an empty space nearby. Razi and Shaili entered a large shop and, soon, Razi began to discuss her favourite cotton designs on display. "Well, this will do nicely, Razi. I'll be working here over the next few years and now I have my special stocks to enjoy too." Shaili said quickly while the two resumed their shopping adventure. An unwilling recognition of the weakened public sphere was evident in many city people. But, Tareni's stoic silence on matters of retribution and reprisal had a profound impact on Razi. "Maybe, we are what we wear, too." She said as the shopkeeper displayed his finest cotton wares. "No, Razi. Organic cotton is the best there is. Look at this design!" Shaili exclaimed with delight and Razi held the fabric looking at it and feeling its softness for a minute. A block away from the arcade, new four-storey office buildings were being constructed with large machine tools lying near the half-finished foundation. A huge heap of concrete sparkled in the sun as if it had passed a litmus test. They watched the construction area for a while and walked to sit on the bench. The atmosphere seemed unbridled, untainted, archetypal despite the structures that paved it like planes on an atlas. "The wheelbarrow is not there anymore," Shaili remarked, almost to herself, as she watched the built environment surround the area with a proud message of advancement.

"Sometimes, the community is held together with adhesives, literally!" Razi exclaimed when the two walked out of the arcade and into the road. Shaili laughed, remembering long-forgotten jokes about binding people together with glue. The arcade entrance behind them was lined with chairs and benches too. They stopped for a minute to look at the area which resembled an ancient citadel unwinding its space with new columns. As they walked away, the people inside the arcade were seen watching them from the windows to ensure their safety on the way home. A car veered away into the road alongside the two and cut through this surreal moment. "Well, my long-awaited trip to

Khumbu will not need inspiration!" Shaili said as they went back home in a changed mood and mindset. "Halse would find Tareni to be unbelievable," Razi replied watching the area for signs of intrusion and damage. The town hall meeting had significantly altered Razi's wavering views on her work in a future that was not predictive yet reasonably unknown. Shaili, on the other hand, had decided to demarcate her daily life much in the way that traditional society in the highlands was known to. The thought of returning to her communal world was fraught with doubt but the day had, yet again, evolved into much more than just Tareni's public space. "I have often wondered if our legacy is a past rather than a question of a renewed ethic. I mean, everything we are and we require is determined in terms like injustice and autonomy. My mother would refuse to make any home remedies because it was neatly categorized by external ideas." She said as they walked past a small medicine shop. The large farm depot next to it was plush with the morning's products and they smiled at each other. "Basically, we have to work towards our goals, not against the wall," Shaili replied in an equally introspective tone. The arcade was a distance away but its motivations were clear, conductive, allayed.

***

"There's been protests in the city, Razi! Come and see." Shreela said over the fence as Razi stepped into the kitchen. Razi walked into the kitchen and locked the cupboards overhead and checked her stove. "Not in Tareni, in the city!" came Shreela's loud voice again. Razi stopped for a second and heaved a sigh of relief. "I am watching television. They have stalled the administration but no violent clashes, they say!" Razi walked over to Shreela's house and watched the television from the doorway without entering the room. There were large crowds in one of the city centres, chanting slogans but it seemed uncharacteristically ordered and scheduled. The two sat on the sofa and silently watched the television broadcast show an assembly take shape. The people were mostly from the city and a few men appeared overly agitated. Razi recognized one of them as the man from the neighbourhood encounter. He was wearing faded clothing and was shouting in a loud but hoarse voice. The moment seemed inordinately still in the room despite the fervour of the protesters as the media anchor panned into the administration building. "How did they reform the assembly in such a way?" Razi asked after a while and went to get a glass of water for herself. "The city was a hub for political conspiracies. They must have found the reason behind the stalemate." She said again and looked at Shreela who was watching the screen with a shocked expression. "I was told yesterday that there would be mass risk if the authorities did not find the right solutions. They are already there." Shreela said suddenly as the media began to report on the regional reformations. "The structures are alright, then." Shreela stood up from the sofa as she said this and poured some fresh juice into two glasses. Handing Razi one of them, she sat down again and asked, "Was the road workable when you were travelling here?" Razi had forgotten about her journey and tried to recollect the exact nature of the road. "Well, I saw many of the places on the way which I had forgotten about." They sat and watched television for a while longer but without the anxiety that was inherent in any public protest. "I must thank you for taking me to the *Nagarpalika* meeting, Shreela.

CHAPTER 9

A working dialogue suits us best." Razi said sipping her juice while Shreela smiled and nodded, reminded of the contradictory predicaments that the nation's leaders were sifting through, decanting, rescinding with fervour.

"The vocational enterprises here are sturdy, aren't they?" Razi asked Shreela after she switched the television off. Shreela looked at her in complete surprise and said, "Yes. The authorities have always supported Tareni's enterprise development. I, personally, would like to see more people build into it." "I've always worked in the city system, Shreela. It's a new ethic here for me even concerning daily work." Razi said and the two of them became preoccupied talking about their livelihood. Stormy surges of economic failure resulting from an aggressive political entropy had caused a fiery shift between the people and governance. As yet, the institutionalisation of reformation ideals had not taken full shape. Razi could see the closure between the city and the nation's larger economic sphere through her move to Tareni. She had been careful, thus far, not to mention it or cause any disturbance. Today, she felt as though the city's protests, shown on television, had played a summary part in unburdening her tired conscience, an erasure caught in the middle, the contrarian identity. Heretical by contrast, the complicity within ulterior forces was a dangerous strain everywhere. Men and women were often known to disappear into the villages without any apparent reason and the cities would then experience a causal void, an inchoate sense, the recurrence of untenable historicity. There was a different method of escape and emergence in Tareni that Razi knew to be lost and archetypal. She, too, had shorn herself from the contrivance in her past.

Early next morning, Razi cleaned her house with renewed zeal, placing the chairs and cushions outside on the sunny veranda. The owner was sure to appreciate her careful handling and home improvements, she thought to herself. A beautiful hand-carved settee that was almost forgotten near the window brought back memories of her childhood home in the lake district. Her cousins would place festival gifts on a similar settee and wait to surprise her mother with them. Smiling to herself, she cleared away the dust and resumed a home life that she had needed for a long time. She looked at the neatly arranged flower pots and saw a colourful but broken planter placed among them as if to say that she was, indeed, free of a damaged and damaging city dysfunction. Mornings in Tareni were near silent with recognizable sounds emanating from the flora and fauna nearby. An unknown and brutalist force was at play in the nation but Razi had felt an equally strong presence of personhood in her new surroundings. She straightened the plants and brushed the veranda furniture. Unknowingly, Shreela and her companions had bartered a new doctrine for Razi which would absolve the present from enmity and weakened thought. The working solidarity between disparate groups could be Halse's happy coincidence too, she thought while dusting and rearranging the living room. An equity was evident and, also, an equanimity that was rare in any social sphere in Nepal. The papers and files on her desk seemed less personal and predicated. She opened the curtains and looked outside her room. The place appeared full and cleared of any wrongdoing. The homes were bright and well-placed. It must be a *Vaastu* principle that had seen Tareni

CHAPTER 9

through those troubled years, Razi thought to herself and stood near the window. A few large trees lined the gravel paths in the distance and she wondered if the ideologies of the past would be reversed or revived. The hills in the far distance did not show any signs of degraded life. Tareni was now, for Razi, a lived, untethered, benefacted experience.

***

Chapter 10

quis custodiet ipsos custodes?

"You will get propositions from the city office and the business community, Razi. I hope you know that. Your work is important for us here too." Devi said over the telephone with Razi listening in sheer surprise. After a muffled cough, she replied, "That's a surprise, Devi. I did not expect this. I am keen to move forward." News of the protests had spread like a wildfire but the town hall meetings and attendant groups were an equalising stability. She finished her conversation and lay down for a nap. At four o'clock, the sharp breeze blew in and woke her up like a timekeeper. A city's hostility and effete relegations had pressed their inevitable marks on Razi and the rest. But, Tareni was a robust invitation and an idyll which Razi had stepped into without much forewarning. Communities around the nation were moving back and forth between ageing problems and solutions that arose at will. The new sense of movement and a decade's turn was different in Tareni. The closeness with the city which many people delved into despite daily annoyances was, still, omnipresent but in a different way. The afternoon rest had made Razi feel the atmosphere's change and dynamism deep in her psyche. Was the world cognizant of the broken realms that had multiplied in Nepal? Razi got out of bed and strode down to the front of the house with a strong gait. What is a true home or is there such a place, she thought to herself and shifted the chairs and plants onto the ledge. The afternoon was nearing a close and, today, it seemed to send out a final assertion to an era of impossible fallibility. The city uproar that swayed society and institutional spheres was deafening yet history's quiet retreat had won a cryogenic margin, an argonaut of simple beginnings, an arc of inverted fallacies. Razi could sense the strength that lay untarnished within Tareni's people. It was a strength that did not fall into popular taxonomy nor did it bear the inevitable scars of anxious messages.

Razi wiped the silver spoons after she washed them and thought about all the family gatherings in the city. Wishing she could meet them here, she put away some more of her belongings into the large kitchen cupboard. The telephone rang again as a curious insertion into this moment of sanctuary. "I'll be coming to Tareni, Razi. The trial by fire here is over. I've finished my work." Halse's loud and boisterous voice deserved applause as he brought the journey to an end. Razi sat on the sofa and sobbed with relief. "I am happy you'll be coming home, Halse. The weather is so fine here." She said hearing Halse laugh at his wife's unusual disquiet. The family histories that had vaulted an era were nearing their retreat too. She talked with Halse for a while and, finally, ended the call with a loud sigh of relief. Many pasts were destined for a quick reprieve in the nation but

Tareni had shone the torch brightly for Halse's return home. His voice sounded lighthearted but there was a change in his temperament which struck Razi as different and balanced. She prepared dinner in a flurry of emotion. Would Halse find his true home here too? Were the skeletal constructs of their past, in actuality, now reversed through Tareni? An undeserved legacy of the nation's woes impounded on their lives had undergone transformation. Now, in Tareni, the reestablished premise of work and communality had arisen as an ethos of a hopeful future. The adherence that had faded due to city criminality was now gathering people together in Tareni for an ideology of strength not weakened power.

As Razi sat outside her house waiting for Halse, the sparrows fluttered in and around the small bushes. She remembered Shreela's comment and looked at them in surprise. There was a small sapling near the entrance that had appeared as though by chance where the sparrows pecked and flew around. A small minibus drove into the lane with the transportation chief in the driving seat and Halse in the front seat. She jumped up and opened the gate as Halse rushed out and gave her a warm hug. "It is so warm and balmy here, Razi. I think we will be home here for a long time." He said in a gruff tone while the transportation chief looked away with tears in his eyes. Razi looked overwhelmed by Halse's surprise visit and laughed as the two men took out his luggage and carried it inside. "Jor was anxious to see me safely to Tareni. He's keeping watch back home too." Halse said as he looked around their new home with sheer delight. "*Dai*, come and have a cup of tea with us," Razi said, inviting the chief into the house. The three city mavens sat in the living room conversing about Tareni and, reflectively, about a long and arduous journey's end called Tareni. "The tea is so fresh." The chief remarked while Halse watched Razi with a beaming smile. Many miles had been won with their journey and many places were now opening to possibilities cautiously demarcated by Tareni's doctrine of good faith. "We have an arcade to sit and rediscover the Nepali lifestyle, Halse. It is a world untold." Razi said with a deep laugh that the two men heard in a surge of emotion.

**